P9-CAB-342

JF GOHMANN
Gohmann, Johanna, author.
Shock and roll

ELECTRIC ZOMBIE

SHOCK AND ROLL

ELECTRIC ZOMBIE

by Johanna Gohmann   illustrated by Aleksandar Zolotić

FOR GEMMA AND HENRY, TWO OF MY FAVORITE
LITTLE ROCKERS. —JG

TO MY DAUGHTER PETRA, WHOSE SILENT
TIPTOEING EARLY IN THE MORNING MADE WAKING
UP LESS PAINFUL. —AZ

abdobooks.com

Published by Magic Wagon, a division of ABDO, PO Box 398166,
Minneapolis, Minnesota 55439. Copyright © 2019 by Abdo
Consulting Group, Inc. International copyrights reserved in all
countries. No part of this book may be reproduced in any form
without written permission from the publisher. Calico™ is
a trademark and logo of Magic Wagon.

Printed in the United States of America, North Mankato, Minnesota.
092018
012019

 THIS BOOK CONTAINS
RECYCLED MATERIALS

Written by Johanna Gohmann
Illustrated by Aleksandar Zolotić
Edited by Bridget O'Brien
Art Directed by Christina Doffing

Library of Congress Control Number: 2018947810

Publisher's Cataloging-in-Publication Data

Names: Gohmann, Johanna, author. | Zolotić, Aleksandar, illustrator.
Title: Shock and roll / by Johanna Gohmann; illustrated by Aleksandar Zolotić.
Description: Minneapolis, Minnesota : Magic Wagon, 2019. | Series: Electric zombie; book 2
Summary: When Zee announces his parents don't want him to be part of the band
    anymore, Fab decides to take matters into his own hands and has a creepy encounter
    with Zee's parents.
Identifiers: ISBN 9781532133626 (lib. bdg.) | ISBN 9781532134227 (ebook) | ISBN
    9781532134524 (Read-to-me ebook)
Subjects: LCSH: Rock groups--Juvenile fiction. | Investigations--Juvenile fiction. |
    Parent-teenager relations--Juvenile fiction. | Zombies--Juvenile fiction.
Classification: DDC [FIC]--dc23

TABLE OF CONTENTS

CHAPTER 1
READY, SET, SEPTEMBERFEST

Fabian Starr lounges on a battered sofa in the garage. His friend Zee sits beside him, lightly tapping some drumsticks against a cooler.

Zee wears his usual black hoodie and red leather gloves. He also sports a pair of dark sunglasses, even though the last of the evening light has already faded from the sky.

Musical instruments are scattered around the garage. Fab holds a red guitar in his lap, absently strumming chords. They watch Emilio, who is demonstrating his latest invention.

"You flip this tiny switch on the side, right?" Emilio pushes his curls out of his eyes and holds up what looks like an ordinary football. "And then this dial lets you decide how powerful you want the shock to be."

Before Fab can protest, Emilio lobs the ball to him. Fab instinctively reaches up to catch it.

"Ouch!" He yelps as a tiny electric shock runs through his hands. He hurls the ball back at Emilio, who also lets out a yip of pain as he catches the ball.

"Cool, right?" Emilio beams.

"Cool. Now, tell me again why I'd want a football that hurts me?"

Fab smiles. Emilio's love of bizarre inventions never fails to amuse him.

"To make the game more exciting, obviously!" Emilio says.

"Because being tackled to the ground isn't exciting enough?" Fab says.

"That was the lowest setting! That wasn't even a big shock. Check this out!" Emilio turns the dial all the way up and tosses the ball to Zee.

The ball almost hits Zee squarely in the face, but at the last second Zee reaches up and grabs it. Fab actually sees tiny sparks spray off of Zee's gloves. But Zee has no reaction!

"Dude!" Emilio shouts. "Didn't that sting?"

Zee sits expressionless. "No. I no feel it. Must be . . . eh . . . malfunction."

"Oh man, really?" Emilio says. "But I had it working perfectly earlier!"

8

Fab studies Zee carefully. He's pretty sure Zee is staring right back at him, though he can't be sure because of his sunglasses.

"She's back!" Emilio suddenly shouts, and they look up.

Their friend Lola coasts toward the garage on her bike. The streetlights cast an eerie glow on her green hair. She looks like a little alien floating toward them.

"Well?" Fab asks. The three boys make their way out of the garage and into the darkness outside.

Lola hops off her bike. "Guess whose band has been selected to play the middle school fair?"

She holds up a large flyer. It reads: *Come one, come all to Septemberfest! Enjoy games, rides, and the music of Electric Zombie!*

Fab whoops. He leaps up to give her a high five. Zee says nothing. Even in the dark Fab can tell he's smiling.

"Whoa. They really want Electric Zombie? They want *our* band to play? And they've already made flyers?" Emilio pulls nervously at his cap.

"Isn't it awesome? When I went by Principal Birnbaum's office they had one waiting for me." Lola grins.

"They sure decided fast!" Fab says. "The audition was only on Monday!"

"Yeah, well. Our competition wasn't exactly stiff," Lola says. "I mean it was between us, that DJ with the awful dance music, or the Marshall twins and their steel drums."

"Still. Our very first audition, and we nailed it! Electric Zombie cannot be stopped! Speaking of awful dance tunes . . ."

Fab pulls his phone from his back pocket and blasts a dance song. He does a goofy, celebratory dance over to Lola. He spins her around. She laughs, shoving him away.

Emilio breaks out into a ridiculous dance. Fab and Lola crack up. They form a circle. "Go 'Lio! Go 'Lio!"

Suddenly, to everyone's surprise, Zee lurches his way into the circle. He moves in the awkward, incredibly slow way he always does.

He has a small smile on his lips. He begins to move his body into a series of slow but complicated breakdance moves.

Lola, Fab, and Emilio look at each other with amusement.

"Go Zee! Go Zee!" they all shout. They gasp as Zee leans down and glides into what has to be the world's slowest, most effortless head spin.

"No way!" Lola shouts.

Fab squints into the darkness. He of course isn't wearing his glasses. Because what self-respecting rocker wears bifocals to band practice?

Fab watches the final revolution of Zee's head spin. He swears it looks like Zee's body doesn't turn all the way with his head. As if his head isn't fully attached!

He quickly looks to see if Emilio noticed this. But Emilio has his back turned and seems distracted by something behind him.

Fab looks to Lola, and her eyes are so wide they look like golf balls. He has a feeling she saw it too.

CHAPTER 2

THEORY OF A ZOMBIE KID

"Yo, Zee!" Emilio suddenly shouts over the music. "Is that your dad?"

Fab turns off the song. Zee swiftly, or at least swiftly for Zee, lowers himself back to his feet.

They all turn. Zee's dad stands on the steps of their house. It is across the street from Fab's. Zee's dad wears the same sunglasses as his son.

Zee's dad mumbles something, but it's garbled, and he speaks so softly it sounds like "Grrkykt."

Everyone stands in awkward silence for a moment. Then Zee picks up his drumsticks.

"I go now," he says, and begins to lurch toward his house.

"'Night Zee!" Emilio calls after him. They watch Zee slip into the shadows of his yard, lurching up the steps and into the house with his dad.

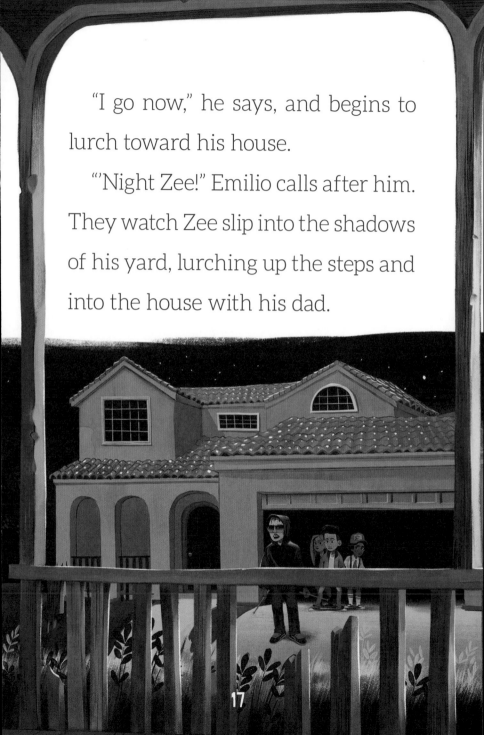

"Was his dad speaking Icelandic?" Lola is still staring at Zee's house, a puzzled look on her face.

"Must have been. And I see father and son still sport the same sunglasses-at-night fashion sense. Man, Iceland must be some weird place, no?" Emilio shakes his head.

Fab says nothing. It's true that Zee's family only recently moved from Iceland. But Fab has his own theories about their peculiar ways.

And it doesn't have anything to do with being from Iceland. In fact,

Fab isn't sure he believes they are from Iceland.

"What about those dance moves?" Emilio laughs. "The world's slowest, most awkwardly moving human, and he breakdances like a pro!"

"For real," Lola says. "That was kind of unreal." She is still staring at Zee's house.

"Yikes, it's getting late." Emilio heads toward the garage to gather his things. "You ready to head, Lo?"

"Um . . . yeah . . ." Lola starts to say, but Fab abruptly cuts her off.

"Actually, Lola, why don't you stay for dinner? My mom always says she never sees enough of you."

"Oh. Really?" Lola looks at Fab, and he gives her a strange look. "Um. Okay. Just let me text my parents."

"Hey, what about me?" Emilio asks as he pulls on his backpack.

"My mom already sees more than enough of you." Fab grins at his friend.

"Ho ho. Hilarious," Emilio says. "Man, I still can't believe we're playing the middle school fair. It's awesome, but it also kind of makes me want to puke, you know? I'm going to have to invent some killer pyrotechnics for this show. In case we, you know . . . suck."

Fab rolls his eyes. "Here we go again. Are you going to worry about us sucking every time we play a show?"

"Of course. Oh, don't want to forget this baby!" Emilio leans down to pick up his football. He lets out a sharp shriek of pain as sparks bounce off his palms.

"Whoa! Are you okay?" Fab shouts. He and Lola rush to their friend.

Emilio rubs his hands in surprise. "Yeah, I'm good. Man, the highest setting is no joke! I forgot I had it turned up." He smiles happily.

"You're happy you zapped yourself?" Lola shakes her head.

"Totally! Now I know it works!" Emilio says. "It's weird that it malfunctioned with Zee. He didn't seem to feel anything." Emilio carefully flips the tiny switch to the off position.

"That is weird," Lola says. She glances at Fab.

You have no idea how weird, Fab wants to say. He knows he has an odd look on his face.

He really needs to talk to someone about Zee. To make sure he isn't crazy. And Lola is the most sensible of his friends.

"Ready for some dinner, Lo?"

CHAPTER 3
IMAGINE ZOMBIES

"I'm so glad you could join us, hon." Fab's mom heaps more pasta onto Lola's plate. "I feel like I hardly see you anymore. Even though I know you're in our garage most nights!"

"You should pop in during practice and say hi," Lola says.

"Oh, I can't! I'm forbidden," Fab's mom says. "I'm not to interrupt the creative process." She gives Lola a wink.

Fab rolls his eyes. "We just need to focus, Mom. Having you out there watching would be weird."

"Well, I'm excited I finally get to see you perform. That's so wonderful you were selected to play the fair!"

Fab's mom reaches over to ruffle his spiky hair, and he playfully ducks away. "Right, sorry. Don't want to mess up the new rocker 'do."

Lola giggles. "Speaking of rocker 'dos, Lola. I love the green hair!"

"Thanks," Lola says. "My own mom isn't quite so in love with it."

"Oh, I think it's so fun! I just love how committed you guys are to your band," Fab's mom says.

"Mom, sheesh," Fab mutters, feeling embarrassed.

"Whatever Fab, your mom is awesome," Lola says. "We can't thank you enough for letting us use your garage, Ms. Starr. And thanks for giving us that comfy sofa. It sure beats sitting in lawn chairs!" Lola twirls spaghetti onto her fork.

Fab's mother waves her hand in the air. "It was just gathering dust in the basement. I'm glad someone is getting use out of it. Oh! I forgot the garlic bread!" She hurries into the kitchen.

"Lola," Fab whispers across the table. "I really need to talk to you."

Lola pauses from eating her salad. The leafy spinach pokes out of her mouth, the same shade as her hair. She swallows. "I thought you were acting weird. What's going on?"

"It's Zee," Fab says.

"Ah. I had a feeling," Lola says.

"So you've noticed it too! I'm not just imagining things!" Fab says, feeling relieved.

"Noticed what exactly? What do you mean?"

"That he's a . . ." Fab starts to say the word, but hesitates. He's never said it out loud before. Now that he's about to, he realizes how crazy it sounds.

"A what?" Lola asks. "A weirdo to the first degree? An amazing drummer? We know those things."

"No! That he's a zom—"

"Here we go!" Fab's mom bustles back in and plunks a bread basket onto the table.

"Thanks." Lola digs in. "It smells amazing!"

"Oh, thank you! I've been experimenting with more baking, and I . . ." Fab's mom chatters on about bread recipes.

Fab stares across the table at Lola. She raises her eyebrows at him like, *What? What were you going to say?*

Fab thinks for a moment. He doesn't want to say it in front of his mother. If he could just give Lola a hint . . .

Suddenly, Fab puts his face into his plate of spaghetti and grabs a mouthful of noodles. He tilts his head to the side, the pasta dangling out of his mouth.

"Braaaaaaaains!" he moans.

"Fabian Isaac Starr!" Fab's mom says. "What in the world has gotten into you?"

Fab quickly sucks down the noodles and wipes the sauce off his face.

"Are you three or thirteen, young man? I don't know if you're trying to impress your girlfriend or what. But I'm pretty sure you know not to play with your food!"

"I was just joking," Fab mutters. "And Lola's not my girlfriend."

He can feel his face turning red. He glances at Lola. He is surprised to see that her face is the opposite of red. In fact, she looks as though she's gone a bit pale.

She understood me, he thinks. *And she knows I'm right! Zee is a zombie!*

After dinner, they clear the table. Fab waits outside with Lola for her dad to pick her up.

A half-moon lights up the sky. Dead leaves rustle over the ground. They stare across the street at Zee's house and the thick woods beyond.

"So," Lola finally says. "You think our drummer is the walking dead."

Fab gulps.

"That explains how you came up with the name for the band. I wondered how you thought of Electric Zombie."

"I know it sounds nuts," Fab says. "But you've noticed things too!"

"Yes," Lola says carefully. "I've noticed that he's from a foreign country and is new in town and very shy. But that, my friend, doesn't make him a brain eater. I can't believe you! You're the one who kept telling us to give Zee a chance!"

"I know!" Fab says. "But I'm starting to get creeped out! His family moves like they're underwater. And have you seen Zee's eyes? They are the freakiest shade of green!"

"Maybe his family has some sort of muscle disorder that makes them move like that. Who knows?" Lola says.

"Anyway, it certainly doesn't interfere with his drumming. He's lightning on the drums! As for his eyes, he probably wears colored contacts or something. I mean this is a guy who wears leather gloves every day! He obviously has his own sense of style."

"Yeah?" Fab croaks. "Well, one night I saw his dad in the woods pushing a wheelbarrow filled with dead animals!"

Lola's eyes grow wide. "Oh, Fab, you did not!"

"I did too!"

"Fab . . ." Lola says. "I think you either really need to start wearing your glasses. Or you need to stop reading scary comic books."

Fab feels a flash of anger. "And I think you know I'm right but are too scared to admit it!"

Lola rolls her eyes. "Fine, if you don't believe me, let's go see what they're up to right now!" He starts to stride over to Zee's house.

"What? No!" Lola hisses. "What are you doing?"

"I'm going to peek in their windows," Fab hisses back. He turns and see Lola isn't moving. "What's wrong? Too scared?"

"No! It's just . . . that's trespassing!"

Fab folds his arms and stares.

"Oh alright, fine." Lola shakes her head.

Together, they creep through Zee's yard. They carefully make their way onto the porch. Fab can make out a dim light coming from one of the windows.

He motions to Lola, and they tiptoe over. His heart pounds. They lean forward, their foreheads almost touching the windowpane.

The room inside is completely empty, except for a rickety wooden chair. In the chair sits Zee's dad.

He wears a tattered business suit, with pant legs that appear to have splatters of mud at the ankle. He of course has on dark sunglasses.

Why would he wear sunglasses to sit in the dark? Fab wonders.

He squints. Zee's dad is holding a jar in his lap. He appears to be popping olives into his mouth.

"Wow," Lola whispers. "Zee's dad likes olives. How terrifying."

Fab starts to feel sheepish. *Maybe Lola is right? Maybe his imagination really is getting away from him.*

But something about the way the light glints off the jar makes Fab lean closer. Suddenly, he freezes. He hears Lola gasp. He turns toward her. She sees it too.

"Those aren't olives, are they?" Fab whispers.

Zee's father digs his hand back into the jar. He pulls out a slick handful of eyeballs, which he pops directly into his mouth.

HOOOOONK!

Fab and Lola jump in surprise. Behind them, Lola's dad has pulled up to Fab's house. He is honking the horn. Lola scurries down the steps and runs toward the car.

But Fab sneaks one last peek in the window, then freezes with fear. Zee's dad seems to be looking right at him!

Fab leaps off the porch and races after Lola.

CHAPTER 4

A BAD INFLUENCE

The next day at school, Fab trudges up the stairs to his locker. He hasn't seen Lola since last night. After she jumped into her dad's car and waved a hasty goodbye.

The whole thing at Zee's house feels like a dream now. He badly wants to talk to Lola and see if she finally believes him.

Fab tossed and turned last night worrying about Zee. For all of Zee's strangeness, Fab really likes his friend. And he loves their band.

If he's right about him . . . what do they do?

Fab passes a large Septemberfest poster hanging at the top of the stairs. *Featuring the music of Electric Zombie!* He pauses to admire it.

"Congrats on the gig. I told you you'd be great for it."

Fab turns toward the voice, and sees Lola's cousin, Josie. She wears a David Bowie T-shirt. Her bright purple hair is in two tiny pigtails.

"We're excited!" He tries to play it cool, but his stomach has filled with butterflies at the sight of Josie.

"Thanks for suggesting we do it. We should give you a cut! I mean . . . if we were going to get paid. Which we aren't. But you know . . ."

Josie laughs. "Don't worry, I won't come looking for my cut just yet. I'll wait until you make it big!" She gives Fab a playful punch on the shoulder as she passes.

His face flushes pink. Fab watches Josie skip down the stairs. For a moment, he feels a bit lighter.

He rounds the corner to his locker. He hums an Electric Zombie song as he rummages for his science book. He slams the locker door closed, and the first thing he sees is Zee's face.

"GAH!" Fab shouts.

"Sorry. It just Zee."

"Sheesh! I didn't see you standing there," Fab says.

He wonders what Zee is doing over in the junior high hall. Zee is

46

fifteen. His classes take place in the high school wing.

"What's up? What brings you over here?" Fab asks. He hopes his voice sounds normal.

"I need talk," Zee says. He has his hood pulled up high today, and his skin looks even paler than usual.

"Sure. Everything okay, buddy?" Fab asks.

Zee leans against the lockers. Fab can't help but notice that even with his strange style and the weird way he moves, he still always looks cool.

Fab leans against the locker, trying to strike a similar pose.

"I afraid not," Zee says quietly. "I am leave band."

Fab looks to see if he's joking. But Zee of course has his sunglasses on. Fab can't really read his expression.

"Huh? What do you mean?"

"I so sorry. You know I love band. But my father . . . he say I must quit," Zee directs his gaze to the floor.

"Why? I don't understand. You can't leave the band! You *are* the band! Your drumming is the only reason we're any good." Fab stares at his friend.

"That kind of you to say. But—"

"What about Septemberfest, Zee?" Fab interrupts, suddenly feeling panicked.

"I know. I so sorry," Zee says.

"Did your dad give a reason?" Fab asks. He anxiously runs a hand through his spiky hair.

Zee says nothing for a moment. "He . . ."

"Yes?" Fab asks.

"He think you are bad influence."

Fab is so taken aback he almost bursts out laughing. *He* is a bad influence? *That's pretty rich coming from an eyeball eater!* Fab wants to shout. Instead, he tries to keep his voice calm.

"Me? What did I do?"

"Well." Zee shifts uncomfortably. "Yesterday he try to greet you. To say hi. And you just stare at him. You no reply. He say that all you ever do. Just stare."

Fab thinks back to last night, when Zee's father mumbled at them while they were dancing. That was a greeting?

"Oh. But, I mean, your dad knows I don't speak Icelandic, right? I didn't understand he was saying hi."

For a moment Zee looks confused. Then his face relaxes. "Ah. Yes. Icelandic. But he was not speaking Icelandic."

Fab gives Zee a long look. *You aren't even from Iceland, are you?* He wants to say. But he bites his tongue.

"I feel bad he thinks I'm rude. What if . . . what if I come over tonight to chat with him, so he can get to know me better?"

As soon as the words leave Fab's mouth, he can't believe he's said them. The last place he wants to be is inside Zee's house with his creepy parents. At night! But he can't let Zee quit the band.

Zee shakes his head. "No. That very bad idea."

"Why? I'll just stop by and say hi. What could possibly go wrong?"

To his surprise, this makes Zee tilt his head back and laugh. Fab realizes this is the first time he's ever seen Zee laugh really hard.

He catches a glimpse of Zee's back teeth. He can only surmise it's been awhile since he's been to the dentist. Some of his molars are a dark shade of gray.

Just then, the school bell rings. Zee quickly clamps his mouth shut.

"No. Very bad idea."

Zee lurches off down the hall, leaving Fab to gape after him.

CHAPTER 5
NOW OR NEVER

Fab stands in his front yard facing Zee's house. The last of the pink sunset has already slipped behind the trees.

He clutches a heavy Tupperware container filled with very rare meatballs. His mom gave him a strange look when he'd asked if she could make the meatballs extra rare.

But she seemed pleased that he was being so neighborly. She didn't ask many questions.

Fab knows Zee and his parents like meat. Especially rare meat. And he certainly doesn't want them to be hungry while he's there.

His phone pings. It's a text from Lola. *Let me know how it goes!* it reads. *Don't let them eat your braaaains . . . LOL!*

Fab gulps. Lola still claims to not believe his theory on Zee. Even after seeing Zee's dad gulp down eyeballs.

She insists there has to be some logical explanation for everything.

She thinks his going over for a visit is a great idea. That Fab will see that they are just a normal, slightly quirky family.

"Alright." Fab sighs. "Now or never."

He slowly makes his way across the street. His palms are sweating, and he grips the Tupperware more tightly.

Just think of the band. Think of Septemberfest. Do NOT think of zombies eating your brains . . .

As usual, Zee's house looks completely dark. Fab wishes he could have come by earlier, when the sun was up. But he knows Zee's dad doesn't get home until later.

Taking a breath, he makes his way up the creaking porch. He raises his hand and gives two gentle knocks. He waits. Nothing.

Considering how slow they are, I could be here until dawn before someone reaches the door, he thinks.

Finally, the door creaks open a couple of inches. To Fab's relief, it's

Zee. Though he doesn't look very happy to see him.

"I, uh . . . brought your parents some homemade meatballs!" Fab smiles nervously.

"No," Zee says.

"N-n-o?" Fab stammers.

But the door is suddenly pulled wider. Fab sees Zee's mom standing beside him. Fab has never really seen her up close. He tries to keep his expression neutral.

Her skin is even paler than Zee's, and her hair is wild and frizzy. She also wears the same sunglasses as Zee and his dad.

"Friend of Zee," she says, her voice raspy. "Come in."

"Um. Sure. Thanks," Fab says, entering the house. She shuts the door. A shiver runs down his back.

The house is so dark Fab needs a moment for his eyes to adjust. As usual, he isn't wearing his glasses. This makes everything seem blurry around the edges.

He glances around the living room. It's completely empty, except for a single cardboard box sitting in the middle of the floor.

"Forgive mess," Zee's mom says. "We no unpack yet."

Fab nods like he understands. Though he doesn't understand how anyone could live in a house for over a month and not even own a lamp?

"Thank you for balls of meat," Zee says. He pries the Tupperware away from him. "You go now."

"But I haven't even met your mom! It's so nice to finally meet you, Mrs. . . . uh . . ."

Fab trails off. He realizes he has no idea how to pronounce their last name. He'd seen it once on one of Zee's school papers. He's pretty sure it didn't contain any vowels.

To cover for the awkwardness, Fab grabs Zee's mother's hand. He gives it a quick kiss, like she's the queen of England. Her skin is like ice.

What am I doing? Fab thinks, feeling slightly mortified. He's never kissed a woman's hand in his life!

Zee's mom lets out a low, croaking laugh. "How nice," she says.

She grabs Fab's hand, and brings it to her mouth. She holds it there for a second. *Is she smelling my hand?!*

Fab waits for her to let go. Then he feels something sharp press into his knuckles. *Are those her TEETH?*

"Beverages!" Zee suddenly shouts. He quickly cuts between Fab and his mom, forcing her to drop his hand.

"Come, Fab. Let us offer beverage refreshment to you. Then you leave, yes?" Fab follows Zee closely

as he lurches down the pitch-black hallway.

Zee's mother creeps along behind them. She makes what sounds like low growling noises. He doesn't dare look behind him for fear he might completely freak out.

He's relieved when they arrive in the kitchen. There is at least one dim light bulb hanging from the ceiling.

Fab gets a look at the room. And he almost wishes he couldn't see. Because beneath the light, sitting in the same wooden chair Fab saw him in the night before, is Zee's dad.

"H-h-hello," Fab says, his voice coming out like a squeak.

CHAPTER 6

MEET THE PARENTS

For a moment, no one says anything. Fab stands stiffly in the shadowy kitchen. Zee and his parents just stare at him.

"Um, how about that beverage, Zee?" Fab forces himself to smile. His heart pounds so loudly he feels certain they can hear it.

Zee doesn't move. "It in basement."

"Oh. Well, you don't have to go to any trouble," Fab says.

"It no trouble," Zee's mom says. "Zee, go get friend beverage."

Zee slowly lurches toward a door, then turns to Fab. "You will be okay?"

"Huh? Of course!" Fab croaks. *Why wouldn't I be?!* he wants to shout. But Zee is already disappearing down some stairs. Fab is now alone with his parents.

"So . . . how do you like the neighborhood?" Fab says to Zee's dad. "Are you feeling settled?"

Zee's dad says nothing. He hasn't moved since Fab entered the kitchen. And Fab can't read anything behind his sunglasses.

Is he even awake? Fab wonders. Small beads of sweat form on his forehead, even though the house is incredibly cold.

"Yeah. Well . . ." he tries again. "I for one am glad you guys moved in. Zee is great. And he's seriously, like, the best drummer I've ever seen."

Zee's parents say nothing. But Fab can hear the mother's raspy breathing. It seems to be getting faster.

Fab turns to her. He blurrily sees that she's moving toward him. She has a giant, crooked smile on her lips.

A scream of panic threatens to rise in his throat. Suddenly, Zee reappears in the basement doorway.

"I back!" he announces, and Zee's mom freezes in place. Zee is carrying a little wooden tray bearing four small glasses. Fab peers at the crimson liquid inside.

"Tomato juice?" Zee offers him one.

"Uh, sure," Fab says, slowly plucking one off the tray.

Zee offers some to his mom, and then to his dad. For the first time since they walked in, Zee's dad shows signs of life, and picks up a glass. *So he is awake,* Fab thinks.

Zee and his parents gulp at their drinks. Fab raises his to his lips. The smell makes him wrinkle his nose.

What kind of rancid tomatoes are these? He pretends to take a tiny sip.

Fab glances around the room, looking for something, *anything,* to talk about. He spots a small sculpture sitting on the kitchen counter.

You don't own a kitchen table, but you make time to display art? Could this place be any weirder? he thinks.

"That's um, an interesting art piece. My mom likes sculpture too."

Fab squints at it with his blurry vision. He tries his best to summon the art terms he remembers his mom throwing around. "It looks very . . . abstract."

The room is quiet for a moment.

"That," Zee finally says, "is raccoon skull."

"Whaa—?" Fab starts to ask, but Zee's dad interrupts, mumbling something in his low, quiet voice. Fab can't make out a word he says.

But Zee clearly understands him. "No, no." Zee shakes his head at his dad. He mumbles something back in an equally low tone.

"Is uh . . . is everything okay?" Fab asks nervously.

Zee turns to Fab. "Yes. He was asking if you are idiot."

"Oh," Fab says.

"I explain that no, you smart boy. You just too cool to wear the bifocal," Zee says.

"Ha! Right! Yeah. I mean, I've got them here, I just . . ." Fab fumbles in his back pocket for his glasses. Then he slides them on.

As he does, Zee's dad comes into focus. Fab can clearly see the yellowish tint of his skin. The crimson splash of tomato juice on his lips. He can't help but think how much it looks like blood . . .

"You know!" Fab suddenly shouts, whipping off his glasses. "I really should be going! But thank you for the juice. And I hope you like the balls of meat, I mean the meatballs, and I . . . good night!"

He bolts past Zee and races down the hallway. He fumbles with the knob on the front door.

Fab shoves his way out. He runs across the lawn toward the warm safety of his own house.

Fab knows he blew it with Zee's parents. But he's so relieved to be out of that scary house, he almost doesn't care.

CHAPTER 7

A BAND'S NIGHTMARE

"Let me get this straight," Lola says. She and Fab are sitting on the couch in his garage, waiting for Emilio.

"Zee's parents didn't have fancy furniture and they offered you tomato juice. And so you raced out the door in a terrified panic?"

"It wasn't that they didn't have fancy furniture!" Fab sighs. "They didn't have *any* furniture! And what about the raccoon skull? Are you just going to ignore that? Who keeps random skulls lying around?"

"Maybe it *was* an art piece. Maybe it's wasn't even a real skull! Or maybe it was just some weird—"

"What? Icelandic custom? I swear Lola. Zee could show up with a severed foot in his mouth, and you'd tell me it's just an Icelandic custom!" Fab shakes his head.

"What do you want me to say, Fab? I'm sorry I don't trust your overactive imagination and horrible eyesight. Might I remind you, you only recently believed there was a yeti living in the woods?"

"That was totally different," Fab says defensively. "That St. Bernard was huge. And I was a little kid!"

"It was only last year!" Lola says.

"Well . . . whatever. It was just because I watched that freaky mythical creatures documentary."

"Exactly! You got some crazy idea in your head and convinced yourself it was true." Lola shakes her head.

"Listen, don't get me wrong. I love that we spent a month yeti hunting. You know I love yetis. But I only love the *idea* of them. Because that's all they are, Fab, a fun idea."

Fab says nothing. He can see Emilio making his way toward the garage. He doesn't want to talk about this in front of him. He doesn't need both of his friends thinking he's loony.

"Hey dorks. Sorry I'm late." Emilio saunters in and glances around. "Where's Zee?"

"Good question," Lola says.

"He didn't show up at school today," Fab says. "And he won't respond to any of my texts."

"What?" Emilio says. He turns to look at Zee's house.

"That's weird. Even for him. He knows we need to practice for Septemberfest. Do you think he's sick or something?"

Fab and Lola exchange a look.

"Let's just go knock on his door. I mean it's right there—" Emilio takes a step toward Zee's house.

Fab quickly shouts at him. "No, Emilio!"

Emilio looks at Fab in confusion. "Why not?"

"I think . . . um . . . I think Zee's parents don't want him to be in the band anymore," Fab says.

Emilio's eyes widen in disbelief.

"What? Are you joking, Fab? But Septemberfest is in two days! What are we going to do?" Emilio says.

"Without Zee we'll suck for sure. There aren't enough pyrotechnics in the world to make us sound good without him!"

"Oh, that reminds me, Emilio," Lola says quietly. "Principal Birnbaum says we can't have any pyrotechnics. It's against the school fire code."

Emilio stares at Lola, his mouth gaping. He flops down between them on the couch and pulls his ball cap over his eyes.

"Wake me when I'm dead," he mutters.

Fab buries his face in his hands. "Ugh! What are we going to do?"

"C'mon guys. It's not the end of the world! Maybe . . ." Lola says. "Maybe Emilio can build a drum machine?"

Fab and Emilio both let out a groan.

CHAPTER 8

GRATEFUL UNDEAD

The next day, Fab and Lola stand at their lockers. Lola peers at a mirror taped inside her locker door.

"Do you think I should dye my hair a different color for Septemberfest? Maybe try a new look?" she asks.

Fab sighs as he searches through his locker for a pencil that isn't broken. "How about we wear bags over our heads as we're booed offstage? That would be a new look."

"Fab," Lola says. "You've got to be more positive! Emilio says he was up all night working on a drum machine. He totally thinks he can get it working in time for the show."

"A drum machine can't hold a candle to Zee. And you and I both know it." Fab slams his door shut.

"GAH!" he shouts. Zee is once again standing right beside him.

Zee gives him a small smile. "I scare you again."

"Yes! Yes, you did!" Fab says, trying to compose himself.

"Hi Zee," Lola calls over.

"Hello Lola friend," Zee says. He turns back to Fab.

"I so sorry for missing practice yesterday," he says.

"Um, it's okay," Fab mumbles. He feels very awkward after what happened at Zee's house. He isn't really sure what to say.

"But I have news that is good," Zee says. "I can still be in band!" He taps his gloves against Fab's locker.

"What? You can?" Fab exclaims. "But what about your parents?"

"My parents fine with it! They like you. Think you are nice young man."

Fab looks at Zee in disbelief. "Seriously?"

"Yes. In fact, they ask me to give you present." Zee reaches into his pocket and pulls out a small black case. He hands it to Fab.

Fab pries it open. His mind races with what could be inside. *Squirrel femurs? Eyeballs?* But no. Inside is a pair of sunglasses just like Zee's.

"They are prescription sunglasses. So you can see, but still be cool rocker," Zee says.

Fab slides them on and blinks. He is surprised by how sharply he can

see everything. It's like he has on his regular bifocals, but everything is just slightly shaded.

"These are awesome!" Fab says. "They're from your parents? But . . . how did they get my prescription?"

He studies Zee's face, which he can now see clearly. In the light of day, Zee suddenly doesn't seem so mysterious. In fact, his expression actually looks a bit shy.

It's the first time Zee has ever made such a friendly gesture to Fab. Fab can't help but feel touched.

"You dropped your glasses in our hall. When you . . . ah . . . did your quick exiting."

Zee reaches back into his hoodie and pulls out Fab's glasses.

"Oh, yeah. Right," Fab mumbles sheepishly. Then he quickly takes them from him.

"My dad able to make for you quickly. He use special glass from Iceland," Zee says. "He invent the glass himself."

"He invented it?" Lola says. "That's so cool!"

"Yes. We have very sensitive eyes, so he make for family. He know a lot about eyes. He is scientist, you know."

Fab can feel Lola shooting him a look. "Really? I didn't know that," Fab says. "Well, thanks! I love them!"

"Good." Zee nods. "Okay then. See you at the practice, my friends." He lurches away, heading off down the hall.

Lola leans against her open locker, smiling smugly.

Fab glances at her. "What?"

"His dad is a scientist!"

"So?" Fab says.

"So! That explains everything! The skull, the jar of eyeballs . . ."

"It might explain why he *had* a jar of eyeballs. It doesn't explain why he was *eating* them," Fab retorts.

"We aren't even sure that's what we saw," Lola says. "It was dark!"

Fab says nothing. He's too busy admiring his new sunglasses in Lola's locker mirror.

She smirks at him. "You are impossible, Fabian Starr. But you do look pretty rad in those glasses."

CHAPTER 9
PANIC! AT SEPTEMBERFEST

"This is humiliating!" Emilio hisses. Emilio, Fab, and Lola are standing onstage in the middle school auditorium in front of a red velvet curtain.

They clutch at their instruments. Lola is on bass, Emilio on keyboard, and Fab on electric guitar. Only Zee's drum set sits empty.

At their feet, a swarm of high school and middle school kids mill around at various booths and games. A small crowd is beginning to gather by the stage.

Electric Zombie was supposed to start playing fifteen minutes ago. But there is no sign of Zee. The students are glancing curiously at them and whispering.

To make matters worse, Fab spies Josie near the middle. She gives him a wave, but her expression looks puzzled.

Lola walks over to Fab. "If he wasn't a zombie before, he's going to be one soon. Because I am going to make him even deader than the undead when I get my hands on him."

"He said he'd be here at four," Fab says. "He seemed fine at practice last night. Maybe his parents changed their minds?"

Emilio makes his way over. "Could he be out on the lawn riding the rides or something?"

"You mean like he decided to ditch the show and is just going round and round on the Ferris wheel?" Lola rolls her eyes.

"Well, I don't know!" Emilio snaps. "It was just a thought!"

Out on the floor, two senior boys walk over to Josie. She smiles at them and chats. She gestures to the stage.

One of the boys looks up at Fab and smirks. He can hear him say something about "just little kids." Fab feels his face grow hot.

"Stay calm! I'll go look for him," he says. He slings his guitar over his shoulder and heads backstage.

He pushes his way through the heavy velvet curtain and peers into the darkness. It looks even darker than usual with his new sunglasses.

"Zee?" Fab calls quietly. He thinks he hears a faint noise toward the back. "Hey! Is that you buddy?" he whispers hopefully.

He creeps through the shadows, closer to the noise. Out front, the rumble of the crowd seems to be building.

Fab slowly makes his way past boxes and old set pieces from drama club. At last, he sees a familiar shape crouched in the corner.

Zee is hunched close to the floor and doesn't seem to hear Fab approaching. Fab is about to call to him. But he suddenly stops dead in his tracks. What is Zee doing?

He squints. Zee has a roll of duct tape in one hand. He is winding it around and around his other hand. A hand that doesn't appear to be fully attached to his wrist!

Fab gasps. It's the same hand that flew off at their last show. *I didn't imagine it! And he's TAPING it back to his wrist!*

Fab stumbles. Zee's head snaps up at the sound. Fab is shocked to see Zee isn't wearing his sunglasses.

He stares straight at Fab. His yellow green eyes almost seem to glow in the heavy shadows.

Fab scrambles away and tries to fumble back to the auditorium. His feet tangle in a small pile of rope, and he suddenly lunges backward.

He falls through the curtain and out onstage. He lands flat on his back, right at Emilio's feet. The crowd roars with laughter.

"Nice entrance," Emilio says, bending down to help Fab to his feet. "We're really knocking this gig out of the park. Hey, you okay?" Emilio stares at him.

"I . . . I . . ." Fab stammers.

"You look like you've seen a ghost," Emilio says.

Close! Fab wants to say. He hurries to the front of the stage to tell Lola what he saw. But then suddenly behind him, he hears a beat.

Fab turns, and sees Zee seated behind his drum kit. His sunglasses are back on. His dark hair flops about slightly as he pounds out the beat of the opening song.

CHAPTER 10

TRIUMPH OF ROCK

The auditorium falls quiet. Fab can feel all eyes on him. He gulps. His mouth feels like he's eaten cotton.

Emilio and Lola rush into place with their instruments. They stand waiting for him to play the opening chord.

Fab's mind is still racing from what he saw backstage. He glances back at

Zee's wrists. But Zee has his sleeves pulled tightly around his gloves.

Zee gives him a small nod. He mouths a single word. "Play."

Swallowing hard, Fab slowly leans toward the mic. As if on autopilot, he strums his guitar. The crowd lets out a small whoop.

Despite how bizarre and confused he feels, he gets the same rush of excitement he felt at their last show. He sings the opening line.

"You destroyed my heart, like a pack of love piranhas . . ."

The band slips seamlessly through their songs. The crowd cheers louder after each one. Everyone on the floor is dancing, including the senior boy who'd called them "little kids."

Zee's hands fly over his drums, his gloves moving so fast they seem to blur. At the end of his drum solo, a girl calls out. "Wooooo! Zeeeeee!"

After their final song, Fab shouts into the mic. "Thank you! We are Electric Zombie!" The crowd hoots and whistles. Fab grins so hard his face hurts.

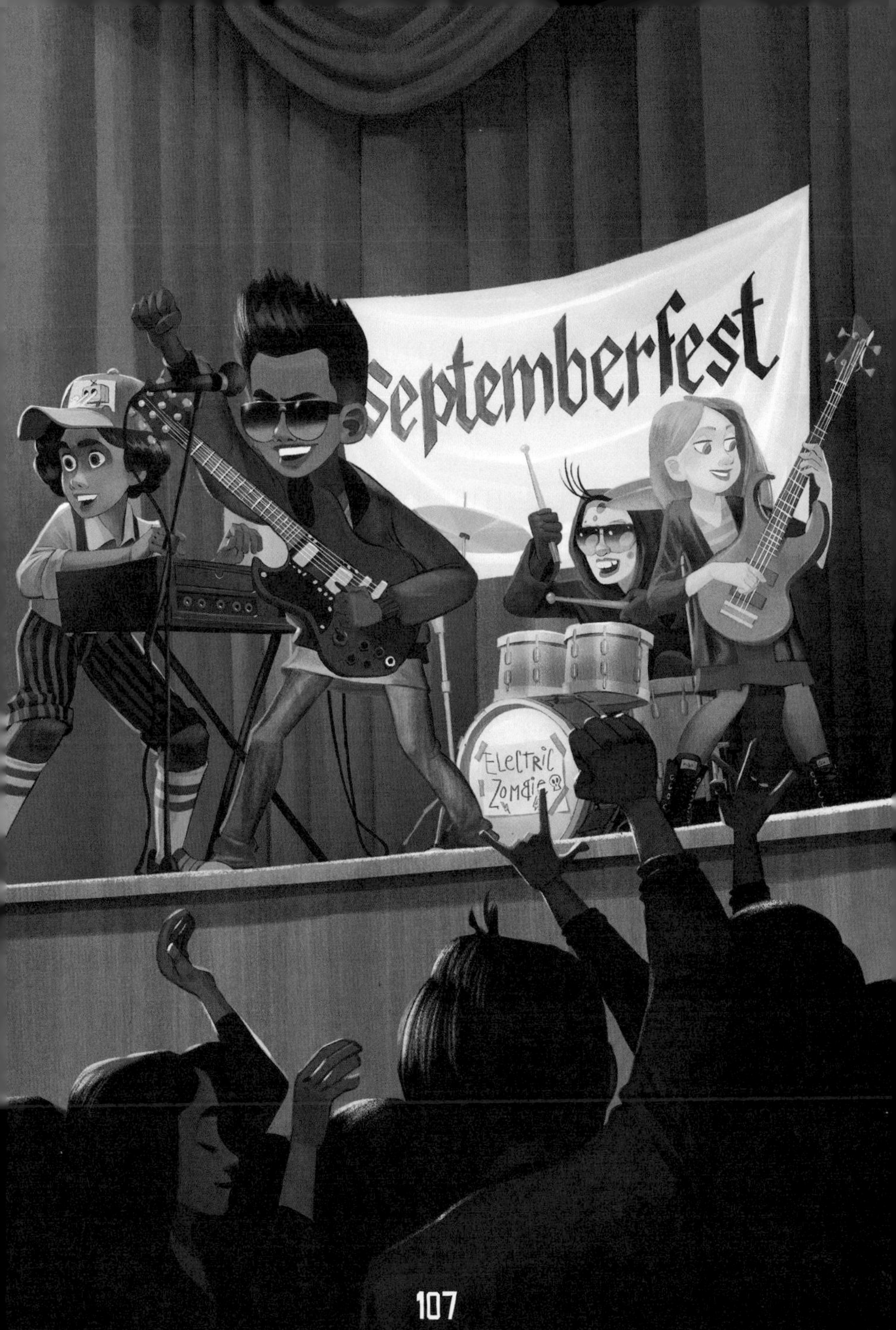
Septemberfest
ELECTRIC ZOMBIE

After the show, the band stands in the parking lot. They are loading their equipment into Fab's mom's SUV. "You were amazing, sweetie!" Fab's mom beams at him.

"Thanks, Mom." Fab smiles.

"And Zee, my goodness!" she says. "I had no idea you were so talented."

"Thank you, Ms. Starr," Zee says.

A group of students walk past on their way to the fair rides. "You guys were awesome!" one girl shouts.

"Yeah, you rocked!" another girl calls over.

"Sweetie!" Fab's mother exclaims. "You already have fans!" Lola snorts with laughter, and Fab rolls his eyes.

"Alright, I'll stop embarrassing you." His mom chuckles. "I'll drive this stuff back so you can stay and have some fun at the fair, okay?"

She gives him a kiss on the cheek before driving away.

"You have a groupie already, Starr?" Fab turns to see Josie and her friends walking toward them.

"Ha! Nope, that's just my mom," Fab says. His face flushes pink.

"Yeah, I figured." Josie gives him a wink, then turns to Zee. "Zee, I didn't think it was possible, but I swear you played even better than last time!"

"Thanks," Zee says. "I put some new tape on my sticks. It help with grip. See?"

Zee holds up his drumsticks. A strip of duct tape is wound around both ends. Zee turns to Fab and gives him an unreadable smile.

Is it possible? Fab wonders. *Was Zee just putting tape on his sticks, not his hand? It was dark, and I did have on my new sunglasses . . . And Zee's hand certainly seems fine now. But . . .*

"You guys want to ride some rides?" Josie breaks into Fab's thoughts.

"Sure!" Emilio says. "That would be awesome."

The group starts to move toward the rides. But Fab and Zee stand for a moment, watching each other.

Zee finally cocks his head to the side, and gives Fab a funny little grin. "Come, my rocker friend. Let us enjoy our Septemberfest triumph of rock, yes?"

Fab says nothing. But then can't help himself. He smiles. "Sure."

Tonight, Fab just wants to forget his brain eater worries and enjoy his friends and their show.

"Hurry up!" Emilio calls back. "I want to go to the haunted house."

"Haunted house?" Fab says.

"Yeah! It's supposed to be crazy scary," Emilio shouts. "It even has a zombie graveyard!"

Perfect, Fab thinks, careful not to look over at Zee. *Just what I was hoping for ...*